Catch of the day

Chapter 1

We Meet Tipton

It was one of those hot, humid Northern nights. The day had been a scorcher with sidewalks hot enough to fry an egg. Southerners migrating

north to the great auto factory mecca didn't expect

such oppressive heat. Of course there were many

things they didn't expect. Mostly they didn't expect

the poverty and the crime. For young boys who had

known little of the Southern country life, the inner

city existence caused no dissonance. The older folks

told of the ways back home but to us this was home

with its housing projects and rows of dilapidated

buildings. With the exuberance of youth we were full

of life and generally undaunted by the ever present

dangers of the city. There were times, however, when

we transiently shared the fright and vigilance which

were our elder's constant companions. Such a night

was tonight. Tommy, Dougie and I stared

motionlessly from the front porch out into the dark

night. We were watching for the evil, scary fellow

who had been following us today. At one point, he'd almost caught up to us, but we had given him the slip by ducking into old man Kirby's grocery, sneaking out the back door, running down the alley, and climbing over the fence through Tyrone's yard around the corner.

"Joey, don't you think we ought to tell mom?" Tommy, my older brother by thirteen months, whispered.

I just shook my head.

Dougie, the youngest, looked up at Tommy. "I'm scared. What if he finds us?"

Tommy's eyes brightened. In the porch light you could see his thin freckled face. His short red hair stood up like a picket fence on his skin and bones frame. "Don't worry, Dougie. He'll never find us here." His reassuring smile calmed Dougie.

"There's way too many people out on their porches for him to spot us."

It was customary for us to sit out on the porch at night hoping for a breeze. The little row houses grew hot during the daytime. Very few people in the neighborhood had even a fan. Sometimes our family of seven and the upstairs family of five would sit late into the night avoiding as long as possible the return to the sweaty indoors. The best times were during or right after a thunderstorm. Such storms always seemed to come late in the evening. The sky would light up in serial splendor, thunder would crash, and Granny would bolt for the safety of the bedroom. Her temporary absence allowed us boys more freedom and we would head for the flooded street corner. Once, Dougie suffered a nasty cut on such an escapade, but he healed fast without infection and was proud of his jagged scar.

Tonight, the street lights glowed heavy with moisture. It hadn't rained all week and the air was sticky. Granny slowed her wooden rocker when she saw the man approaching the house. He wore a helmet and carried a billy club. She couldn't see his badge and tell that he was a policeman until he reached the porch. She sighed with relief.

"Ma'am", the young patrolman began, "I'm officer Tipton. I'll be assigned to this area all summer. You may have heard that there was a breakout at the prison. They shot the warden and headed toward this section of town. One of them is Pudgy Hawk. His picture was in all the papers last year when he tried to collect that ransom. He was foiled by some foolish kids who beat him to the ransom money, set an old bird trap for him, and landed him in the slammer. Rumor has it that he's out to get these kids. I think he's going to try to hide out here for a while then slip across the Middleburg river into Canada. We've had our eye on his cousin, Sawtooth Fats. He has been in and out of every jail from here to Chicago. He also spent a lot of time at A.J. Olmes, the school here in town that houses juvenile delinquents. My point is, he knows a lot of bad apples."

He continued, "if you hear anything about these ex-cons, you can reach me at the station down the street."

Now that his official business was stated, Tipton took a moment to joke with us kids.

"Caught any catfish lately on that cane pole in the corner? Bet you boys are afraid of those giant night crawlers we have around here!" He grinned

broadly and made snake-like movements with his

hand.

"We ain't 'fraid of nothing," I said under my

breath. But he heard me and just smiled. Suddenly,

he grabbed one of my hands and prepared his cuffs. I

didn't flinch.

"Oh, do me mister, do me!" shouted Dougie,

holding out both of his stout nine year old wrists.

Patrolman Tipton accommodated Dougie and

even gave him the key to uncuff himself. Granny

took advantage of the moment.

"I told you boys that if you didn't behave, I

was going to call the police. Ha, ha. Guess you'll

mind me next time. Take 'em away sonny. Lock

them in the slammer. Say, sonny, you're awfully

young to be a police officer."

Officer Tipton walked over to Granny, sitting there in her large, terrycloth robe sipping a cola. Edentulous, her lips appeared puckered. Rows of wrinkles lined her face, and she squinted to get a better look.

"Well, Ma'am, I'm new around here but I've been walking the beat on the North side for almost four years."

The sudden gunshots down the street shattered the folic. Tipton sprinted away. The cuffs still dangled from Dougie's wrist. We played with them until Granny scooted us off to bed. Tipton hadn't returned and there had been no sign of the stranger. The next day the neighbors told us Tipton had tripped on that old, rough section of sidewalk, plunged head first and grazed himself with a bullet from his drawn revolver. As for the stranger, he was to reappear soon enough.

Chapter 2

Last Year's Escapade

Early the next morning we resumed our usual routine. We headed for the Middleburg River with fishing rods, baseball, glove and bat. All summer, dawn to dusk, we were on the move. Curious and energetic, we were also keen observers and resourceful.

Although we had a bowl of cereal before leaving home, we stopped at the "day-old" bakery for a snack. The doughnuts were stale but inexpensive.

As we munched the stale doughnuts, we continued on out way to the river and Tommy began talking about the previous day.

"I've been thinking. Do you suppose that Pudgy guy the policeman was talking about is the one who was chasing us? He was fat and had a big nose. He sure looked mean. And when he spotted Dougie's "Davy Crocket" hat he started acting really strange. I think he would have tried to grab us there if it hadn't been for Mr. Penny.

"Yeh," I chimed in, "Mr. Penny is a great neighbor to have. It's not every day that one can have an ex- pro boxer at your favorite fishing spot. When that stranger started glaring at us and coming toward us, Mr. Penny looked him square in the eye and said, 'Hey mister, you'd better get lost before you get hurt.' Well that stranger left right away but I guess he must have been hiding behind those bushes waiting for us to head towards home."

Then Dougie spoke up, "I sure was scared when he pointed that gun at us and told us to march. Boy, did we scatter. Those squishy worms and dirt Joey threw in his face gave us a good head start."

"Yeah, and we really gave him the slip in Kirby's store", said Tommy.

We walked slowly along the highway. Near the river, there were six lanes of traffic. It was only 6:30 and the morning traffic was light. Dougie spotted several empty "pop" bottles and added them to his bulging knapsack. He had to cram them in because there wasn't much room among the necessities he carried. He always had his pocket knife; marbles, matches, tootsie rolls, Al Kaline baseball cards; jacket, vanilla "doughballs" fish bait, ball and glove, extra nylon and hooks, and a few old sparkplugs (good for sinkers). Today, of course, he also had a pair of shiny handcuffs.

My duffle contained an old wool army blanket, a dozen comic books, a small hatchet, canteen, peanut butter and jelly sandwiches, and a chunk of cheddar cheese.

Tommy carried a small switch blade, compass, and a white "rabbit's foot" for luck. He carried the baseball bat and three fishing poles. In the small pocket of his jeans he carried some rolled up bills.

We crossed the highway and settled in at our favorite fishing spot. We spread the blanket. Nearby was a place for a fire and a fish fry. Tommy stood and spoke again about the stranger.

"How would he know that we were the ones that found that money last year? When we saw that butler leave the bag right there on Belly Island, we didn't know who it belonged to. It was funny when that guy who started chasing us pitched right into that little pit covered with leaves and branches. His leg was caught in the noose just before he stepped into the hole. I bet we could have caught one of those wild ducks or rabbits if he hadn't messed up our trap."

"Maybe he saw Dougie's Crockett hat," I offered and then regretted that I'd said it.

"Lots of kids have those hats!" shouted Dougie, not wanting the blame and feeling a little hurt.

"Ok, you're right," I said. "But something must have put him on to us. I wonder how he figured out who we were."

"Maybe we will never know the answer to that," said Tommy, adding, "Do you think we should have told Mom or Granny?"

"No, they'd make us turn in the money," I said.

"Well Joey, it's not really our money, you know," said my elder brother.

Of course, he had never wanted to turn in the money either, even after mom had read the story in the paper about the kidnapping. Mom had almost cried. Granny said it was that picture of the cute little four year- old boy that was upsetting. The newspaper article described how the four year- old had been found in the woods safe and sound right near where the ransom money disappeared. I guess it made mom worry that an awful thing like that could happen to one of her kids.

"What do you mean, it's not our money?" I snapped. "Of course, it's ours. Finders keepers, losers weepers." Besides, we earned the money. We found little Scotty, untied him, gave him some food, gave him some M&M's, and told that policeman where he was just in the nick of time." I reminded my brother.

Tommy was unfazed. He just looked at me with that "give it a break, kid" look of his.

Dougie wasn't quite ready to give up the argument.

"When are we going to spend it? I want a shiny, new, red Schwin Bicycle with a horn and light and mud flaps. Dougie's eyes lit up as he spoke."

After Tommy's look, I knew there was no sense in arguing and said, "I don't guess we can spend it, Dougie."

"Why not?" he pleaded.

"You know, It's for Granny."

"All of it?"

"Yea."

"All ten thousand?"

"Yes, Dougie," said Tommy. "You know Granny has to have that operation. If she doesn't, she could die. She can barely walk up the stairs by herself. The doctors said her heart has a really bad valve. I know Granny doesn't seem to pay it much mind, but it sure worries mom."

Maybe there will be some left after the operation." Dougie beamed as he thought about what the "leftovers" would buy.

"Probably won't be any left. If there is we have to turn it in. Wouldn't be right to spend it," Tommy said with an older brother's sense of authority.

Dougie and I looked hard at our older brother. We still didn't totally agree with him. But this was not the time to start a big argument. Besides, we looked up to him and he was the leader.

"I guess we better walk over to Belly Island later today and make sure that no one has discovered where we hid the money. Granny might have to go to the hospital any time now." Tommy said seriously.

Chapter 3

Captured

We spent most of the day fishing and enjoying the sunshine. Later in the day, we stowed some of our gear in a hidden tub near our fishing spot so we could travel lighter. It was about three more miles to Belly Island and it was by now already three o'clock. A little food, water, and our knives were the essentials.

Also, a folded piece of plastic was stuffed into my jacket pocket.

Taking the shortest route, we followed the river's edge 'til we reached the old folks home, then climbed the steep embankment and peered over the water to the island. We continued around the edge of a small, private airfield where, in places, the weeds were as high as Dougie's head. The old, seldom used path led past a burnt, abandoned cabin. Shortly, we emerged into a small clearing just underneath the concrete bridge to the island. Circling under the bridge, we hardly noticed the hot, pungent odors and the discarded rubbish that always greeted us there.

Suddenly, we heard two men shouting. We quickly hid behind a pile of old tires.

"You're loco, Fats."

"I tell you, it will work, Hawk."

"Man, you're going to land us back in the slammer. Those cops are hot on our trail."

"Those cops are stupid, Hawk."

They would never look for us back at Kirby's store where those kids gave you the slip. Those kids are bound to show up there sooner or later. We nap 'em, scare 'em to death, and find out where our money is. Then we head for Canada."

"You're crazy, Fats. I hear that cop Tipton is one smart cookie. You can bet he's keeping an eye on that storefront. And our pictures are plastered all over that section of town. We got a bounty on our heads. We gotta get out of this city. Forget those fool kids. We'll get them when the heat is off. Remember we got the rope."

"I want the money, Hawk. How do we know those kids haven't spent it? The heat won't die down for more than a month. Our money may be long gone by then. I say let's find those kids and make 'em talk or string 'em up with their own rope. Ha, ha, ha," he roared.

Fats dangled the rope in front of Hawk and read the inked-in name: "Dougie, yes Dougie Jones, Belvedere Street."

Now they both began to laugh uncontrollably.

We huddled silently. The mention of Dougie's name sent a shiver down my spine. We had all forgotten about the inscription on the rope that had tripped up Pudgy Hawk.

I thought the men were leaving, and I stood up. I fell right over one of the tires and landed with a thud. In a moment the two men had seized us. They tied us up in a knot and led us toward their little motor boat.

"Well, well, well, talk about some luck. Looks like we'll both get what we want. As soon as we get these brats back to the boathouse, I'll get 'em to talk. I'll feed 'em to Freddie one at a time if I have to," laughed Hawk.

"Who's Freddie, Mister?" Dougie cried.

"You'll see," and he kept laughing in that mean, maniacal manner.

Chapter 4

Freddie

Blind folded and tied all together, we pitched about in the back of the motor boat. After what seemed like hours, we were herded from the small boat to a much larger one. As they lifted us, I managed to lean back and look out the bottom of my blindfold. I saw in bold letters the sign: "Billy Island Harbor" posted on the rough dock beside us. On the side of the larger boat I saw the inscription, "Floating Angel". The white letters stood bright against the peeling red paint.

Once inside they shoved us into a little room. We heard the door being locked. Dougie was the first to twist loose from the ropes, and he quickly untied us. There was a porthole on the side wall and a small ventilation duct in the center of the ceiling. We didn't see any other openings. The room had a peculiar odor. There, beside us, almost to the ceiling, were stacked plastic bags full of marijuana.

"Tommy, look at all that weed," I said, amazed at so much.

"Yea, these guys are really crooks. We gotta figure out a way to get out of here," Tommy said as he paced back and forth eying every inch of our little prison.

Dougie didn't understand. "How come they got a boat full of weeds?"

"It's grass, Dougie," Tommy said quietly, his eyes still roaming the room.

"Grass?" Dougie was still puzzled.

"Mar-i-jua-na," instructed Tommy, saying each syllable slowly and emphatically. Dougie's eyes grew as big as saucers and he stammered, "People smoke this?"

Tommy nodded.

Meanwhile, I peered through the porthole as the boat headed around the northern rim of the island. I could see the old abandoned sawmill growing closer and closer. I wondered to myself. "Where do the logs float from to get to this sawmill?" I had often seen ice floes moving down the cold Middleburg River in the winter. Occasionally the river froze and it was rumored that at such times one could drive a car across the ice to Belly Island. I still couldn't picture logs floating down the river. Suddenly I began to imagine that the boat we were on was a big log on its way to the giant saw. I could hear the creaking and groaning of other huge logs and the buzzing of the saw was deafening. In a few moments the image passed but I still felt hot and sweaty.

Trying to maintain my composure, I whispered, "Hey look. There is that old sawmill where Uncle Elmer used to work. Maybe we can build a raft and escape." I didn't really think that we could build a raft without tools. Besides, we would be locked up or worse. Nevertheless, I wanted to encourage my brothers. I tried to smile.

In the next few hours, we found ourselves locked in a small room inside the now abandoned sawmill.

The "Floating Angel" had been docked in a hidden cove beside the sawmill. Just before the docking, and in the nick of time, we had donned our blindfolds and wrapped the ropes around ourselves giving the impression that we had been tied up the entire time. We were hustled into our new prison which was a room about 12' by 12' with bars on the only window. The window looked out on the cove where the boat was hidden.

From the muffled voices in the adjoining room it sounded as though there were five or six men. We could smell the strong aroma of freshly brewed coffee and baked pizza. The latter was indeed a torture given that we were famished. By now the sun was setting and there was a slight breeze. The men were talking excitedly and it sounded like they were planning something big. They kept talking about some bank and some old school. It was hard to hear through the door and we couldn't make out a lot of the words.

Tommy and I were still shaking from seeing Freddie. Dougie didn't appear to be the least bit affected. Just before we were taken inside the sawmill, Hawk and Fats had stopped us. They had pulled down our blindfolds and started laughing uncontrollably. There before us was a large enclosure surrounded by a thin wire mesh. At one end was a small gate. At that spot there were the scattered ruminants of an unfortunate creature (perhaps a chicken). Near the center of the enclosure was Freddie. The six- foot long crocodile was sprawled out in the dirt. He was motionless. Was that a smile on his long crooked snout, I thought to myself.

Then the two men had begun to taunt us.

"Hey, you little runts, there's Freddie. Ha, ha, ha. Look at those jaws."

Hawk continued, now singing: "come on ol' Freddie, get yourself ready for a meal that's better than meat ball and S'getti."

The whole scene had shaken me and Tommy and we looked away from Dougie so he couldn't see the fear in our faces. Dougie had already decided that Freddie wasn't alive. Dougie didn't even think he was real. But if he was real, he was certainly dead. Not even his stomach was moving.

Once inside the small sawmill room, Tommy and I began to regain our composure.

"We have got to make a plan!" said Tommy.

"I'm hungry," exclaimed Dougie.

"Maybe one of us can escape," I said.

Escape. That was a nice idea.

I could squeeze out through the bars (If we could bend them a little). Then I could creep away from the mill and find my way back to the marina. There I'd call the police. Tipton could come and rescue us. I'd sure like to get out of here before they decide to make me a meal for Freddie, I thought.

I had always been a daydreamer. Now I imagined myself at the helm of a shiny coast guard ship sailing into the hidden cove. Now I was rounding up Hawk and his gang. I wore a new commander's hat and carried a sharp, silver sword. The thugs were groveling before me. I had them placed in chains in the galley and made them row the ship all the way to the prison. I could see Fats struggling with each row of the oar. He was panting. Sweat was pouring down his forehead. I was merciless. I kept saying, "keep it up, Fats, or I'll make you walk the plank."

There I was, staring out the window. I hardly noticed the magnificent moon over the horizon. I was lost in reverie. A big smile covered my face.

Chapter 5

A Rival Gang and Escape

A sudden "bang" jarred me back to reality.

"Sounds like somebody got shot," whispered Tommy.

Another shot rang out. Then we heard a series of shots in rapid sequence. Bang. Bang. Bang. Outside the building there was an explosion. Then we heard the sound of a large, truck-like engine. It grew fainter as the vehicle moved toward the woods.

Night was falling and the building was very quiet. No longer could we hear any voices. A low moaning sound was coming from somewhere. It didn't really sound like it was coming from the next room, but we figured that it had to be there or right outside.

The door was closed tightly and we couldn't budge it. We kept looking around the room and out the window for a way to escape. The night was still. Stars filled the sky now. The moon was almost full and rising. The breeze was getting stronger.

A few minutes later, we heard the truck noise coming from the direction of the woods. Then there was a commotion next door. Someone let out a loud moan and it sounded like something was being dragged across the floor. The truck noise again faded.

Maybe fifteen minutes later, the men returned.

A loud voice said, "Good work, Salty! Too bad two of them got away. Anyway, looks like we cleaned up pretty good. I don't think this gang will give us any more trouble. Kingpin will want to move some of his men over from Chicago and take over this operation."

"But boss, what about those two guys that got away?"

I'll leave a man outside in case they show up again. One of them was busted up pretty good. They must really know these woods well because they sure disappeared."

Hey Boss, Kingpin said to be sure and eliminate the one they called Fats. You suppose any of these guys we took care of were Fats?"

"Beats me. They all looked fat. That's why we could sneak up on them. They were all sitting around "feeding their faces."' This place is a pig sty.

"Hey, Boss."

"'Hey' what? If you don't quite bugging me with 'hey this' and 'hey that', I'll close your trap permanently."

Salty had found the map diagramming the bank, the school and the tunnel between them. But after his boss's sharp words, Salty just shrugged his shoulders and dropped the map. At least it appeared that way through the key hole.

"Have you guys looked around this place real good? What's behind that door?

In a moment someone was trying to turn the doorknob of our prison. We huddled behind the door.

"It's locked, Boss," a voice said.

"Oh, forget it. We've got to make tracks. We have to get this boat and all these drugs on the way to the kingpin in Chicago."

We saw the boat leave. Again, it was quiet. Outside we could see the fireflies and one constant red glow. Tommy said the red glow was a cigarette being smoked by the guy left guarding the mill. We were afraid to make too much noise because he might hear us. Wearily, we sat quietly on an old mattress in the corner. We ate our remaining bread and cheese. Dougie wished that he had his usual supply of tootsie rolls and so did I. Fortunately, we did have some water in the canteen which had been stuck into one of my jacket pockets.

The next thing I knew, it was almost daylight. I'd been awakened by some noise. Or was it a dream?

I'd thought I'd heard someone calling out. But it was quiet now and I wasn't sure. Tommy and Dougie were still asleep. I walked quietly over to the window. There was no sign of the guard and I didn't see or hear anyone. I fumbled around in my pocket for my knife. One of the bars was very rusty at the bottom. I worked my knife back and forth, back and forth along the edge. What I really needed was a crowbar or a hacksaw. Gradually, however, the bar weakened and I could move it a little.

The way the building was constructed, we were partially underground. Outside, the grass was almost up to the level of the window. In fact, I could reach out and touch the grass. It was wet with morning dew. I rubbed my hands across the wet grass. It felt good to touch and nice to stretch my arms out through the bars as if I were free. Suddenly I recoiled in panic. Crawling along the building outside was Freddie. He made a rustling sound in the tall grass and was moving rather quickly. He must have gotten loose during the melee last night. He stuck his huge snout between the bars forcing me back away from the window. From his force, the bars creaked and groaned but held. I was glad that I hadn't loosened them anymore than I had.

The commotion awakened Dougie and Tommy. They both let out a yell when they spotted Freddie (especially Dougie, who later said he thought he was dreaming). Perhaps their screams annoyed Freddie. For a few moments he appeared agitated and bit at the bars. Then he moved away from the window and parked himself about ten feet away.

Now we began in earnest to try to open the door. No amount of shoving, banging, or pounding did any good. We looked around the room for some tool such as a screwdriver or hammer. The room was rather barren except for the old mattress which was actually quite comfortable. The blades of our pocket knives didn't fit into the keyhole and weren't sturdy enough to unscrew the rusty screws holding the door hinge in place.

About the time that Freddie appeared ready for another charge, Tommy remembered that he had an old skeleton key in the secret compartment at the bottom of his rabbit's foot. Dougie and I automatically crossed our fingers and said "come on key, work," as Tommy poked at the lock with the key. Finally, it caught hold and the lock turned with a pleasant click.

We crept into the main room. It was large with a high ceiling. The early morning rays of the sun came through a large window and made the sawdust in the air glisten. The room was a cluttered mess. Blood stained the sawdust covered concrete floor. We found the maps lying there. Mention of Olmes School perked our interest. That was my old school.

It felt good to be free. Tommy jumped up and clicked his heels together. Dougie tried unsuccessfully to do the same. We all laughed a little, and then we remembered about Freddie. We decided that we had to be careful. We found Dougie's rope which Fats had dropped. We also confiscated some cans of soda from an old frig in the corner. The cans of tuna fish were too old and rusty looking even for three very hungry boys.

Carefully, we peeked out the door.

Chapter 6

Grounded

Freddie wasn't so smart after all. He had returned to his enclosure. Tommy quickly ran up and closed and latched the gate. Then we headed for the woods and made our way to the harbor. From there we crossed a bridge and ran the rest of the way home. It was still early, only 7 am. The smell of bacon greeted us at the door.

Mom and granny had been worried sick. They had called Tipton the night before and he had been looking for us the entire night. Shortly after we arrived home, Tipton came by to tell our folks that no sign of us had been found. He was delighted to see us. He was glad to get a bacon biscuit, too.

We told Tipton all about the kidnapping we had just been through. Except we didn't mention the map we had found or our previous run-in with Pudgy Hawk the year before.

Tipton pieced together the bits of information provided by each of us. He decided that Fats and Hawk had escaped the rival gang's surprise attack and were hiding in the woods somewhere. He said he'd be going back to look for them. He borrowed our phone to call his chief.

Even though we protested that it wasn't our fault, we were grounded for a week. It seemed much longer. We occupied ourselves with monopoly, marbles, jacks, and library books. The end of June was nearing and the days were long and hot.

Finally, when mom lifted our "being grounded", we went to a Saturday matinee to see a Three Stooges movie. We sure liked the buttered popcorn. We laughed all the way home when Dougie tried to make noises like Curly and Moe.

Mom found an article about three men being killed at the old saw mill site. We read their names: Toaster Jones, Red Morton, and Hot Shot Sweeny. There was no mention of Sawtooth Fats or Pudgy Hawk.

Chapter 7

Tipton Shines

For the next few days we returned to our summer ritual of baseball, fishing, and long walks. The annual speed boat races were a major attraction of the summer. The crowds disrupted our usually peaceful park, but we had some consolation in that we collected an extra number of discarded pop bottles. One week we had so many empties that we had to go to several different grocery stores since some of the local merchants regarded us and our bottles as a nuisance. While the crowds stayed and the boats made high waves which ruined our fishing, we entertained ourselves by walking along the beams of a new department store foundation. We perfected our balance by going higher and higher each day early in the morning before the work crews arrived. The old discarded nuts and bolts we found there would make good sinkers for fishing off the rocks where one often got snagged and snapped a line. After one morning when Dougie almost fell off a beam 30 feet high, we decided to quit our balancing acts. We decided to take more long walks until the boat racing season quieted down. So, for the next several days, except for early morning fishing, we stayed away from the river. Of course, the entire family was planning to go to the river with a picnic for the big Fourth of July races.

Almost every night we saw Tipton walking his beat. Often, he would stop and ask if we had seen any sign of the men who had kidnapped us. We hadn't. Once he said that if he ever had a family, he'd be proud to have some boys like us. Sometimes he would tell us fish stories about the big ones he had caught. More often his stories were about the ones who had gotten away, especially those in Canada where the cold water sent a chill right through one's wading boots until the whole body was shaking

Mom didn't seem to care much for Tipton, but Granny certainly liked him. Tommy told us that mom always hoped that dad would come back some day from California. His leaving her and us kids like he did made Mom distrusting of men.

Mom didn't completely ignore Tipton. She did thank him for walking by every evening and keeping an eye on things. Our getting kidnapped had made her very jittery. However, she was still optimistic about life and looked forward to the future when times would be better. She was a tall, thin lady with a narrow waist and dark brown hair pulled back behind her ears. She was thirty- three years old but could pass for being much younger. Her big green eyes and smooth skin made it easy for people to warm up to her.

Mom had lost some of her Southern hospitality in this neighborhood. Even before the kidnapping, she had been scared. I think it really started that time an angry, intoxicated man came to the door. He was acting belligerently. When mom started to close the door, she noticed that he had his foot blocking the way. She didn't panic. Cleverly, she said she had to call her kids home since it was getting dark. When he stepped back, she slammed the door right in his face. Then he was really mad. He kept pounding on the door and shouting. He must have looked in the window and saw granny coming at him with her shotgun, because he sure hightailed it down the street. We were just getting home from the park that day and saw him running down the sidewalk with his hands covering his head for protection. Granny claimed that she would shoot any varmint that tried to hurt her daughter. Granny's mother had traveled across the country in a covered wagon in the pioneer days and Granny had some of that same spirit in her. Even with all of her teeth missing (or perhaps because they were missing) she could place a finger in each corner of her mouth and let out a whistle that made the hair stand up on a person's neck.

Tonight Tipton was beaming with pride. Mom had seen his picture in the paper and the article about how he had helped to capture some hoodlums from

Chicago. His left arm was in a sling and he had a large bruise on the left side of his face. Still, he had a big grin. He mentioned something about a promotion. He even looked older and more distinguished now. Somehow, his badge seemed to shine more brightly. With a gleam in his eyes, he said:

"How would you boys like to go to the Fourth of July races with me? I've got the day off. I can get us a great spot for a picnic and maybe even get us a boat ride.

Granny and mom looked at each other and smiled.

"Well, we were all planning to go for the day, but granny hasn't been feeling well lately so that would be very nice if you would take the boys," said Mom.

Tipton looked disappointed like he had wanted mom to go too. He tried not to show it.

"Ok then, I'll pick you boys up at 8:00 a.m. sharp on Saturday morning. Right now, I'd better get moving. I've got a lot of pavement to pound," he said proudly.

"Oh, Tony, congratulations on your promotion," Mom said, as he was leaving. We'd never heard her call him Tony and didn't quite know what to make of that.

In our book, patrolman Tipton was okay, but nothing like our dad. Our dad seemed to know how to do most everything. He could repair just about anything around the house including the stove, refrigerator, washing machine and of course the car, He had a green thumb especially when it came to growing tomatoes. He loved to fish, play baseball, play games, and wrestle with us all the time. He was good at cooking fish and most other things but sometimes he did burn the pot of beans when he forgot they were on the stove. He had told us that he had to go to California to find work and that he would be back someday. We believed him and were anxious to show off many of our new skills when he returned.

.

Still it would be nice to go for a boat ride. Maybe we could sit in one of those speedboats before the races. My favorite was the dark red one with "Winston" written on the side. I'd heard that riding in one of those boats full speed would really take away your breath.

Chapter 8

The Hospital

I noticed as the summer got hotter and hotter, Granny seemed to grow weaker and weaker. Sometimes she would hardly get out of bed until late in the afternoon. Then she would stir around some. Mostly, during the day, she would lie propped up on two or three pillows trying to read some book or magazine. She didn't like to be disturbed much anymore either. It was less and less frequently that she would have us sit around the living room floor and tell us about times when she was a little girl and what the world was like then.

"Really, Granny?" we would exclaim when she described her chores back then. She'd laugh whenever she would tell us that by the time she was Tommy's age she was cooking supper even though she had to climb upon a stool to reach the pot of beans on the stove. And gathering firewood was one of the easier chores. Kids nowadays sure had it easy. She'd ask us to imagine washing our clothes with a tub and washboard and, oh yeah, that was after we had drawn the water from the well, hauled it to the house, and heated it on the wood stove.

"Why didn't you have a gas stove?" Dougie would ask.

Just last summer Granny had been so different. Her garden had been well tended. The tomato vines were stalked in neat little rows. The green beans, squash, and okra sprang up next to the cucumbers. No weeds were to be found. This summer only a few cucumber plants could be found. They were surrounded by weeds. Granny had tried to tend her garden but just didn't have the strength. She'd get out of breath. Her legs and feet would swell. After a short time in the hot sun she could hardly move. She wasn't the best about taking her medicine either, but lately she had to, to keep from having so much trouble breathing.

All day Thursday, Granny had looked more pale than usual. She even tried to do without her snuff; but dipping snuff was an old, ornery occupation and a hard habit to break. For dinner, Granny only sipped some soup.

In the middle of the night, mom called an ambulance to take granny to the hospital. Mom said granny was breathing real fast ad talking out of her head.

The county hospital was full of patients. Many of them were poor (indigent was the hospital term used). We had only gone there a few times and then usually to the emergency room.

Once, our little sister had meningitis and went there. Mom said she counted about thirty needle sticks all over little Betsy's body the day after admission. Fortunately she recovered, (The doctors told mom that "it was amazing that Betsy suffered no adverse sequela from such a devastating illness." Mom translated the fancy language to mean that Betsy was lucky to be normal again.)

Kids under twelve were not allowed in certain parts of the hospital but we just quietly walked down the hall to granny's room. The room seemed so white. The walls, the sheets, and even the floors were white. Everything was so clean also, but it smelled to much like cleaning solution.

Granny looked better. Mom said the doctor gave her a large bolus of lasix. We didn't know what a bolus was but figured that the medicine had helped.

They said that granny's aortic heart valve was leaking worse and would have to be replaced soon. Generally, they used a mechanical heart valve, but the doctors said in Granny's case they might consider using a pig's valve. I thought to myself, "If this wasn't such a serious occasion, we could really have some fun with the idea that granny might become part "pig"."

Later, Mom said they didn't do such surgery at the county hospital but maybe Granny could be transferred to the university hospital where patients often went if they didn't have good private insurance. The best insured patients went to the well known private hospital, St. Mortans.

We figured that the doctor wouldn't listen to us if we told him that we had the money to pay for granny's operation. We'd just send him some money in a big envelope and tell him we had more than enough to pay for granny's treatment so please send her to the best hospital.

We left the hospital and walked straight to Belly Island.

Five hundred dollars was more than we had ever seen at one time. In fact, we had never seen a hundred dollar bill. When we looked at one, Dougie said., "Why should Benjamin Franklin get to be on a hundred dollar bill and George Washington only on a one dollar bill? Wasn't Washington the father of the country?"

Even Tommy couldn't answer that one.

When Tommy pulled those new one hundred dollar bills out of the sack hidden in the tree stump, they made a nice crisp sound. I wanted to take some more out just to hear the sound they made, but Tommy wouldn't let me.

Carefully, we replaced the sack and covered it with dirt and leaves. Tommy clutched the envelope containing the $500 and we went home to write a letter to the doctor.

Dear Dr. George Smith,

We know our Granny is sick and needs an operation. She doesn't have any money, but we do. We are sending you some. We have plenty more. Please help Granny.

Tommy, Joey, and Dougie

We asked mom the address of the hospital and carefully folded the money into the letter. After licking the envelope shut we asked mom for a stamp so we could "mail a letter to the hospital".

"Why, that is sweet of you boys to send a letter to your grandmother," she said.

"We do miss her," said Tommy, concealing the envelope.

Chapter 9

The Old Schoolyard

Tommy was beginning his growth spurt and all of his pants rode up to the top of his socks. He still managed to squeeze on his favorite pair of tennis shoes. Although Mom said she expected to see his big toes sticking right up through the shoes very soon. Tommy remained strong and fit, but this new growing made him look awkward as though his arms and legs were too long for his body. The three of us were a sight parading around the neighborhood: Tommy's red hair and freckles and lanky frame, Dougie's Crockett hat and rosey cheeks, and my thick-rimmed glasses and favorite pair of miniature overalls with the pockets stuffed.

We still had the map that the crooks had left at the old sawmill and we were especially intrigued by the mention of A.J. Olmes School next to the bank. The map showed a tunnel leading from the school to the bank. Olmes was my school. Sure it was on the other side of town and I was bused there, but it was my school just the same. My brothers went to different schools from me. It was a peculiar system. Up to the fourth grade we all went to Scrippes Elementary School. That's where Dougie went now. Starting with the fifth grade we were bused somewhere. The system was very crowded, so in alternate years the students were bused to Olmes and Homer. Tommy went to Homer and I went to Olmes.

A.J. Olmes wasn't like most grammar schools. The upper floors were locked and housed juvenile delinquents except in the summer when the school was closed and the juveniles were sent to "summer camp". Some of the kids in our neighborhood ended up there. I went to the public part of the school. We could sometimes see groups of delinquents being placed on buses. They looked sullen and dangerous with all the guards keeping them lined up. My classmates and I would joke that some of us would be sent upstairs before the year was over. I hoped it would never be me.

I had fond memories of the school yard as my brothers and I walked there that hot July morning. I had only been at the school for a year, but I relished the recess periods where we ran wild, endlessly playing Red Rover, Red Rover. Someone from one team would choose a person from the opposite team to come over. Then we would all chant "Red Rover, Red Rover, let Billy (or Johnny or whoever we chose) come over." The kid whose name was called would make a mad dash toward the opposite line and try to break through. Usually, I could break through the opposite line, but sometimes I had to pick out a weak link where one of the smaller kids stood. Once, I almost had my neck rung when two of the larger boys raised their hands at the last moment. I drove under their arms and escaped injury but had to take my turn over again. That time I hit their clutched hands square with my shoulder and busted through the line.

In the winter when it was very icy, sometimes the playground would be one, big, frozen rink. We would run full speed and slide on our feet, or our bottoms or our backs. I would later attribute one of the permanent knots on my head to a particularly good slide which ended at a fence post.

Chapter 10

The Cleaning Ladies

One of my favorite parts of the schoolyard was the antiquated fire escape. It was just a long tube leading from the second floor of the school down to the school yard. From a distance, the outside looked like a giant vacuum cleaner tube. It was round and hollow in the middle. We were not allowed to play in it when school was in session. Today, we were able to enter it, look around, and climb up slowly until we reached the top. If it had been brand new, it would have been much darker inside. There were little worn places where tiny holes at the seams let the light enter enough for us to see our way. At the top, there was a leveling off and we could sit comfortably and peer out one of the little holes to the schoolyard below. There was a little door which led into the school. Usually it was fastened tightly, but today it was slightly ajar. We squeezed in.

Walking around the dim hallways of an empty school is eerie. There are a lot of shadows and dark corners. It is so quiet except for the old building sounds, the creaks and groans of time. Whenever we reached a turn in the hallway, we would stop and listen. Eventually, we made our way to the ground floor of the building. I pointed out my homeroom. There, Mr. Stanton had made us write over- and over again:

"I will not misbehave in class."

We peered through the glass door. The row of seats sat empty. The well- worn student desks were full of hand-carved initials. From our vantage point we could see underneath several of the old-fashioned desk chairs. The little, dark mounds protruding from the undersides reminded me of the times when I had to hurriedly discard my gum before Mr. Stanton got to my row for his daily gum check. Anyone caught might have to stay after school. Sometimes a first offense led only to a knuckle rapping with the ruler.

The noises coming from the boiler room down the hall startled us. We had thought that no one was around. Cautiously, we moved along the hallway. Outside the boiler room, there were two janitor carts full of supplies. Each contained a large wastebasket. By now the noise had stopped. Then we heard footsteps. Two old ladies, wearing uniforms, appeared. Their shirts had "Beacons Janitor Service" written on them. From behind, their shapes reminded me of Hawk and Fats. It wasn't until I heard them talking that I knew it was the crooks dressed up in a disguise.

"Let's get out of here, Fats."

"Yeah, we've done everything except blast through that last section of concrete that leads up to the bank vault."

"We can do that tomorrow evening when all the fireworks are done exploding."

"Yeah we'll have some exploding of our own then."

"We can leave these here carts in the hall and use them to transport the loot out of here."

"By the time the bank opens on Monday, we will be over in Canada. This time we'll just drive the truck through the tunnel since Beacons has a company there too. They'll never suspect our trash bags are full of money."

We crouched motionlessly in the doorway shadows as they walked past, obviously proud of their scheming.

"Yeah, Fats, once we pull this off we'll be on easy street."

"Not even that smart cop, Tipton, will suspect us. By now he's probably found our tracks leading straight to that little quicksand pit over by the old saw mill."

"Yeah, by now he thinks we're goners, the way we stepped backward in our own tracks after we threw our hats into that quicksand was really smart."

"And it was convenient that Johnson left his work truck parked outside while he went on vacation for the fourth of July."

"Yeah, when the cops find his truck, they'll think he pulled off that job."

"Seems logical since he works here."

"Let's head over to Sally Sue's for some food. We have a big day ahead of us tomorrow."

We watched them as they moved down the hallway. They looked funny in their wigs and white gloves. Fats cracked a joke and exaggerated his hip movements as if he really were a woman.

After they had left and we heard the truck pulling away we felt safer. We busted out laughing about the way they had looked in their "git ups".

Chapter 11

Stanley

We explored the boiler room and found the passageway leading to the bank. The entrance was night behind a little door in one corner. The passageway was part of the older sewer system. When we looked at the map again, we saw how the passageway led from the school to the bank. Luckily, Dougie had a flashlight in his pack and we could see well enough to walk down the narrow passageway. It was full of insects and a couple of rats scurried away when they saw our light. Along the way we passed a section that contained a manhole cover high above us. It was lighter there and we could see the rungs of a ladder leading upward. Dougie wanted to climb up to see if he was strong enough to push up the manhole cover. Tommy and I dissuaded him because we had more important things to do.

Further along, there was a passageway off to the right with several stairs leading up to a narrower passageway. A large tool box sat on the top of the stairs along with discarded pop cans and sandwich wrappers. There were even more insects in this section. We could hear the squealing of rats as they scurried about.

"Boy, I wish we had Old Tom, the alley cat," I said. He'd make those rats scatter. Remember that time when Kerchival's German Shepherd got loose and started after old Tom. Suddenly Old Tom whirled around, got up on his hind legs with his tail stiff as a board, let out a hiss, and sent both claws tearing right into that shepherd's face. That dog put his tail between his legs and took off and even jumped the fence back into his pen!"

"Shush! Quiet," said Tommy, holding his finger to his mouth.

"Cut the light," he continued, "someone's coming."

As unbelievable as it seemed, an old hobo, with a knapsack over his shoulder, limped along, talking to himself.

"Stanley, Stanley, you can't be a mole all your life. You gotta get back on those boxcars and head for California."

We tried to remain motionless behind the toolbox. There wasn't much of a place to hide and the old man spotted us.

"Hey, what are you kids doing down here in the dungeons? Don't you know this is a dangerous place? Look at these bites on my leg from one of those rats." He pulled up his pants leg as he said this.

We stared at a gnawed area on his leg. The leg looked funny. It was smooth and hard looking.

He struck his leg with his cane and laughed and said "Don't look so worried boys! It's a wooden leg. I lost my real leg during the war. Just had it plumb blown off. I'm lucky to be alive."

"Do you live down here, Mister?" asked Dougie.

"No, Sonny. I just come down here where it's cool when we have those hot days. Don't nobody bother you down here. The hoodlums are afraid of the rats down here."

"Want a sandwich, Mister?" asked Dougie.

"Thanks, Sonny."

His trembling hands clutched the sandwich and he started walking away.

"You kids better not stay down here too long. It can get real scary at night," he offered as his parting words.

After the old man had left, we figured out that the bank wall must be night there at the end of the smaller passageway which appeared to have been freshly dug out. Curiously, we opened the tool box. There were hammers, chisels, short handled shovels, an axe, a pick, and a stick of dynamite. The box was very heavy with handles at both ends. We couldn't budge it. We noticed that it had wheels on one side, but we couldn't tip it over either.

"So, they're going to rob the bank tomorrow," said Tommy.

"Looks that way," I said.

"Maybe we should call Tipton?"

Why don't we stop them, Tommy," I said.

"How?"

"I've got an idea. I'll tell you when we get out of this creepy place."

"Okay, let's go!"

On our way in, we hadn't noticed that several small passage ways joined the main tunnel at sharp angles because of the way the light shone from the flashlight. On the way back to the school, we could see these little tunnels, damp and full of cobwebs. I was glad to get back to the school and climb the stairs and find the fire escape and slide down without any hesitation.

Chapter 12

The Winston

Later that night, we sat on the front porch hoping for a thunderstorm. I elaborated on my plan. My brothers were skeptical bur agreed to sleep on it.

On Saturday July 4th, I awoke with a start. The dream was vivid. The old man in the sewer was skewering a large rat over a big fire he had built in the tunnel. He kept spinning it around and around. He was singing:

"They eat dogs in China but in Middleburg we have…."

His voice trailed off before he finished and a whole colony of rats came charging at him. He started swatting at them with his cane but there were too many of them. Then I woke up.

It was 5 a.m. and I didn't feel tired anymore so I went to the kitchen to get a glass of water. The house was quiet. Everyone else was asleep. I made myself a peanut butter sandwich and re-checked my bag to make sure I had a pair of pliers and the handcuffs as well as a sturdy piece of long, thin wire.

Tipton met us promptly at 8 a.m. His knobby knees poked out beneath his Bermuda shorts. His legs were ivory white from always being in his uniform.

He had on a red polo shirt and a white cap. He looked more like a taxi driver than a policeman. His sunglasses balanced on his nose and he grinned from ear to ear. The best part of his attire was the long, white tennis shoes he wore, size 13 he said. His skinny legs and long feet made him look awkward.

Fortunately, Tipton had connections. He had arranged for us to get a close- up look and even sit in one of the most famous of all the racing boats, the Winston. It was too early to start the engine so we couldn't actually go for a ride. We settled for sitting in the cockpit and looking at all the control buttons. The smooth, sleek edges glowed in the morning sun and my imagination ran wild. I dreamed of skimming over the water and making one sharp, dangerous turn after another, sending huge waves toward the shore.

It was fun watching the boat races that day. Tipton told us all about each of the boats. He explained how the driver had to be very careful or else in a turn he could lose control and the boat would turn up on its' side and could even explode.

Tipton knew a lot of people. A lot of them recognized him even in his hat and sunglasses and without his uniform. For a while, two pretty ladies stopped and sat with us and kept whispering and giggling. They both liked Tipton and each of them gave him a hug and a kiss on the cheek before they left. One of them asked him if he was coming over later and he said he was. Tommy poked me when he heard that. Tommy was starting to notice girls, but I certainly didn't want to hang around with any.

Tipton bought us hot dogs and sodas until I thought my tummy was going to burst.

After the last race, we started home and had ice cream along the way.

Mom thanked Tipton profusely and told him that Granny was doing better. The doctors had decided to send her to St. Mortons for her operation after all. Mom knew she couldn't afford it, but just that very day the doctor had called and said that the surgery expense had been taken care of. Mom was thankful. She was glad that society helped take care of poor people. We knew otherwise and didn't say anything about the reply we had gotten back from Dr. Smith.

Chapter 13

The Trap

Shortly before dark, we set out for the Olmes schoolyard. When we arrived, we saw the Beacons' truck parked outside the back door. Carefully, we crept up to the door and strung our wire across two small posts about ankle high. We hoped this would be sufficient to trip one of the crooks if necessary. Then we quietly made our way up the fire escape and down around the stairway to the ground floor. Carefully, we proceeded toward the boiler room door. It was slightly open and the janitor carts were nowhere to be seen. Further down the hall, we could see the exit sign at the door where they planned to escape.

Silently, we went about our tasks. After spreading a thin coat of oil on the hallway floor and strategically placing several dozen marbles over that in a section that was quite dark, Tommy crept though the boiler room doorway. Dougie stood guard in the hallway and I searched for another janitors' cart.

By now, it was dark outside and the early firecrackers began to explode.

I'd located another cart and rolled it down to the boiler room. Tommy said the coast was clear so I rolled it into a dark corner of the room.

Near the small door leading to the tunnel, we saw the two janitor carts from the other day. They were identical to the one I had found. The door to the tunnel was slightly ajar and just big enough for a man to stoop down and go through. Unlike the long tool box, the carts were too tall and wide to fit through the door. The door was made so that it swung outward toward us. There was a latch that could be fastened from our side if the door was completely shut.

Soon the firecrackers outside became more frequent and louder. Then we heard a loud explosion from the direction of the tunnel.

"They've blasted through the wall to the bank," said Tommy, "Quick, lets' get in the corner behind the cart."

We took up our positions and waited.

Soon, Fats and Hawk begin bringing armfuls of bags loaded with money and putting them into one of the large janitor carts.

After a couple of trips, Hawk said, "One more trip should do it. That vault wasn't as full as I expected, but we should have a couple hundred grand here. We won't be needing this other cart here."

With that, he gave the second cart a hard shove sending it flying straight in our direction. It crashed into the cart we had placed in the corner and tumbled over spilling bathroom cleaner everywhere. Tommy had quickly placed his hand over Dougie's mouth when he saw the cart flying toward us. Fats and Hawk would have probably heard Dougie's muffled cry if it had not been for the loud voice coming from the tunnel at the same moment.

"Yahoo, Yahoo!"

It was Stanley. He had found the hole into the bank vault.

"That sounded like that old coot we saw here the other day. We better take care of him before he messes up our plans. Let's tie him up and leave him in the vault."

However, by the time the two men returned to the vault, Stanley was nowhere to be found. They could hear him singing but they couldn't tell where it was coming from. They shined the light in both directions along the main tunnel but didn't see any sign of him. The singing was growing fainter now, but they could still make out the words repeated over and over again:

"My ship has come in

My ship has come in

I'm off to California again

I'm off to California again."

As soon as Hawk and Fats had returned to the tunnel heading for the bank and looking for Stanley, we had rushed to the small door and tried to close it. It was stuck open. We shoved and shoved. It seemed like minutes, but it was probably only seconds. Time seemed distorted. Finally, it moved and almost closed completely. We couldn't quite get the latch closed. It didn't seem to line up properly. All three of us were still pushing and at the same time Tommy was trying to lift the door a little bit so the latch would line up and we could get it completely closed and stick something in to fasten it. (the hasp). While we were still pushing, we heard the two ex- cons returning. They were cursing because Stanley had gotten away and they didn't like witnesses. Through the still partially cracked door, I could now see the men getting closer.

"Why did you close that door up there, dummy?"

"I didn't close the door, Hawk. I thought you did."

The two men broke into as much of a run as the small tunnel, the money bags, and their fat stomachs would allow.

I really thought they were going to reach the door before we could fasten it. At the last moment, with the three of us pushing with all our might the lock mechanism lined up just enough for me to jam the handle of the pliers into the lock, securing the latch.

The two men knew that they were trapped. They kept pounding against the door like wounded animals. The lock mechanism was sturdy, but each time they would hit the door the pliers would slide up a bit. I tried to press down on the pliers but it was no use. I just knew that soon the pliers would slip out completely and the door would fly open. That would be the end of our summer fun; no more baseball and no more fishing. We'd probably end up in the janitor carts or worse. By now I was mentally timing their attacks on the door. I'd relax for a moment and then hold real tightly just before the next bang. Tommy and Dougie seemed to instinctively do the same. We were all scared.

"We could make a run for it," said Tommy.

"If only Tipton were here," said Dougie.

Hearing Tipton's name made me think of something.

"Dougie, please get those handcuffs out of my bag," I said, "Hurry, give them to me."

Only about an inch of plier handle held back the two hoodlums. One more stiff shove against the door and it would burst open. By now, they had figured out it was us kids from all our shouting. For a few moments they stopped plunging against the door and tried to convince us to open it for them.

"Hey boys, come on let us out of here. We're not going to hurt you. We'll even give you some of the money. You'd like that wouldn't you? Just think of all those toys and candy you could buy with a bag full of this."

Of course, we were not convinced.

Their talking gave us just enough time. With Tommy's help, I slid the open end of a handcuff down through the lock and snapped the handcuff shut securely in place.

"Whew," I said, exhaustedly.

The sweat was pouring down my forehead and burning my eyes. I wiped my forehead with the back for my hand.

Hurriedly, we rolled one of the janitor carts from the corner over next to the passageway door. Then we rolled the one full of money down the hall to the janitors closet. This was all just in case they were able to break down the door.

Tipton later told us that, as it turned out, they were never able to break down that little door. Trying to escape through the bank, they set off an alarm. They were hurrying toward the van with their arms full of money when the squad cars spotted them. Fats and Hawk were too exhausted to try to run for it and surrendered without a fight.

They wouldn't tell the police what really happened. They kept on saying they had just found the money lying out on the sidewalk. Even under the hot lights of the interrogation room, Hawk and Fats denied knowing anything about the tunnel. And they certainly didn't know anything about the rest of the money. What they were doing dressed as cleaning ladies, they wouldn't say.

Chapter 14

Discovered

We had managed to get home late Saturday evening and slip into the house without awakening anyone. We had left a note for Mom saying we would be over at Uncle George's and not to worry. We hoped that she hadn't called him.

Early the next morning, we headed for our favorite fishing spot.

Dougie had just landed a big carp when Tipton found us. Tipton had watched from a short distance as Dougie struggled with the fish. Tommy and I had offered to help him, but Dougie was determined to catch this one all by himself. The tip of his rod bent almost in two. The cane pole would have snapped, but Dougie had the fiberglass rod. With skill unexpected in a nine year old, he worked that fish. He reeled for a few moments, then gave some slack, then pulled and reeled some more, then gave slack and so on until the fish gave up the struggle.

Tommy and I were admiring Dougie's fish as Tipton walked up.

Tipton was in his uniform today. His spit shined shoes glistened in the sun and his dark blue uniform appeared starched to his slender frame.

"Now, that's what I call the catch of the day," he said, pointing to Dougie's fish. "In some parts of the world, folks would consider that fish a delicacy. Over in Europe, carp is served at banquets."

Then Tipton looked at us very seriously and said in a stern voice, "You boys have been holding out on me. I think you know a lot more about what's been going on lately. One of my associates found my old pair of handcuffs securing a door latch near the boiler room at Olmes School."

"You mean the cuffs we were playing with that night?" I said, trying to act surprised.

"Yeah, those very ones," he said gently.

I thought about saying that we had lost them or given them away, but the hurt look on Tipton's face was too much for me, as he continued, "Once the press gets wind of this story, they'll think I had something to do with the robbery, especially since there is still a lot of money missing. There will be a full investigation. I might lose my badge for letting you kids keep those cuffs. I came back for them once, you know. When your Granny said what a grand time you were having with them, I just reported them lost."

"Okay, we don't want you to get into any trouble. We'll tell you the whole story," said Tommy, speaking for the three of us.

Tipton listened closely as Tommy told things from the beginning: from how we had accidentally stumbled upon the money a year ago up to the events

of the evening of the fourth of July. At certain points,
Tipton would politely interrupt.

"You hid the money in a tree trunk and you
didn't spend any of it for a whole year?"

"That's right."

"And when you opened some of the money, it
was for your granny's surgery?"

"Yep."

"And you planned to turn in the rest of it."

"Yes, sir."

Tipton beamed like a proud father when we
told him about the struggle with the lock and the
pliers and the handcuffs.

He was surprised when we told about hiding
the cart full of money in the janitors closet. No one
had yet discovered the money.

After finishing our story, we all looked directly at Tipton.

He tried to form a little smile but said sternly, "You boys should have told me about all of this before. You could have gotten hurt really badly."

Honestly, Tipton didn't seem to believe the part about Stanley and said that he'd have to look into that some more.

"You boys will have to appear before the judge. Keeping that money you found was against the law. I hope the judge won't be too hard on you."

"Don't tell Mom," said Dougie.

"What about the money we spent for Granny's operation?" I asked.

Tipton shrugged his shoulders and said thoughtfully, "I don't know what is going to happen about that."

Chapter 15

The Judgment

Almost six weeks had passed. With fresh haircuts, we sat before the judge. Our Sunday best clothes felt stiff and scratchy. Mom was beside us. Granny was there too. She'd gotten out of the hospital a few days ago and looked much better. Her surgery and hospital stay had been long and complicated, but now she was making a nice recovery.

By now, the judge had been well informed about the entire case. The press had gotten hold of it. A series of articles had been written. All of the bank's money, except about two thousand dollars, had been accounted for. One reporter kept referring to this two thousand dollars as Stanley dollars. However, no one had found out anything definite about Stanley. A number of street people had sworn that they had seen him and that by Monday he was somewhere in California.

Both the bank and the family of the rescued little boy had offered rewards. The amounts exceeded the cost of Granny's surgery but not the entire hospital bill. The medical community had been in an uproar over Dr. Smith's apparent involvement until it was revealed that Dr. Smith had not pocketed any money, but had given it all to charity.

Both Fats and Hawk had been photographed in their disguises and pictures had appeared in the paper. I still laughed whenever I thought about the way they looked. They had been sent up to the maximum- security prison for recalcitrant criminals.

The judge was a short, little man. His long, black robe almost reached the ground. When he walked into the court room, everyone had to rise.

The judge sat down behind his high bench, pounded with his gavel, and stared down at us. He had a thin, red beard and penetrating eyes. Mom said he was in his fifties, but he had a boyish look about him. Now His eyes sparkled as he began to speak.

"Ladies and gentlemen, we have a most unusual case before us today. I've examined all of the facts in this case very closely. Usually what I see before me in this juvenile court is a kid who is rebelling against his parents and society. He's broken in somewhere and stolen something or maybe hurt someone. He has usually been truant from school and made poor grades. He can't get along well with others."

"The facts in this case reveal some trespassing and some concealing of and spending "stolen" money. However, there are some extenuating circumstances which I've had to consider. I believe these young men have had honest motives. None of them have had problems at home or school. True, they haven't had the parental supervision they need. Still, they live in a home where they are loved."

"In my judgment, it would be a mistake to send these boys to reform school. On the other hand, I cannot ignore the seriousness of this entire matter. Therefore, I am placing these boys on probation for one year. If they break any laws during this next year, I'll be forced to sentence them to time in reform school."

"Officer Tipton Has been appointed by me as their special probation officer, He will periodically give me a report on their behavior. If necessary, I'll have them appear before this court again."

"Do you kids understand?" he asked firmly.

We nodded.

"Okay, court is adjourned," he said with a smile.

I thought he winked at us as he walked by in his long robe.

Chapter 16

Here We Go Again

Tipton continued to be a good patrol officer. He was a good probation officer also. We had settled down a bit after the stern warning from the judge. It was about time for school to begin anyway.

Dad had heard about us and wrote a long letter saying he would be home before long. Granny didn't put too much stock in that though.

The nights were getting cooler now and we needed a jacket to sit out and watch the stars.

I was still a daydreamer. Already, I began to dream about next summer and the adventures we would have. I was determined to build a raft next summer and see where it would take me.

About the time that school resumed, Tommy showed me the short article he had found, quite by accident, on the back page of the paper.

It read: Two convicts are reported missing and believed to have drowned in Middleburg Lake adjacent to the Brushy Prison work site. Authorities found only the hats belonging to Pudgy Hawk and Sawtooth Fats. No bodies have been recovered.

I looked at Tommy and Tommy looked at me.

I said, "think they really drowned?"

"Sounds too much like that quicksand stunt."

"Maybe they are really dead."

"Maybe."

I thought to myself, "Oh brother, here we go again!"